BEARS IN THE NIGHT

by Stan and Jan Berenstain

COLLINS

BRIGHT and EARLY BOOKS for BEGINNING Beginners

Trademark of Random House, Inc., William Collins Sons & Co. Ltd., Authorised User

13 15 17 19 20 18 16 14 12

ISBN 0 00 171271 3 (paperback)
ISBN 0 00 171210 1 (hardback)

A Bright and Early Book for Beginning Beginners
Published by arrangement with
Random House Inc., New York, New York
First published in Great Britain 1972

Printed & bound in Hong Kong

In bed

Out of bed

Out of bed

To the window

At the window

Out the window

Out the window

Down the tree

Out the window

Down the tree

Over the wall

Over the wall

Under the bridge

Under the bridge

Around the lake

Under the bridge

Around the lake

Between the rocks

Through the woods

Out the window

Down the tree

Over the wall

Under the bridge

Around the lake

Between the rocks

Through the woods

Up
Spook
Hill!

WHOOoo!

Down Spook Hill
Through the woods
Between the rocks
Around the lake
Under the bridge
Over the wall
Up the tree . . .

In the window!

Back in bed

WHOOOOOO